The Magic Fairy Door

Laurie Ingersoll

D1377519

Dedicated to K, M, J, S and the
imaginative kid in all of us.

A trio of kind fairies
is looking for a home.
Across the fields they've traveled
to call a place their own.

They hope to find a family
where they can join right in,
a happy welcome household
where their story can begin.

Lexie is the eldest,

caring for the rest.

Always neat and tidy,

her manners are the best.

You'll often hear her singing,

but you have to listen hard.

She loves to read and write

whilst lounging in the yard.

Daisy is the middle.

There's no guessing what she'll wear!

She's often quite disheveled

with wild bright red hair.

She's a budding artist,

painting each and every day

using bright, happy colours,

keeps the clouds away.

Boo is the little baby,
she loves anything that glows.
You'll find her wearing sparkles
from head down to her toes.

The garden is her playground,
with flowers, birds and bugs.
She loves to bring them goodies
and gentle little hugs.

One day when Lex was reading
about a magic door,
the fairies got to thinking.
They wanted to learn more.

This door could let them enter
the world of girls and boys,
so they could play together
and share their games and toys.

What would children be like,
besides from being tall?
Would they enjoy the fairies,
so fragile and so small?

Or would the kids be frightened
and want to run away?
The only way to find out
was to search that very day.

The fairies flew for miles,

over meadows, hills and streams.

For anyone so tiny,

space is bigger than it seems!

At last they finally saw one,

a tiny rose pink door.

The three sneaked up in silence,

this new door to explore.

Lexie gave her approval,
and Daisy nodded too
then looked for their sister,
but where on earth was Boo?

She had stopped to hug a bee
who was buzzing in the grass.
Then they all were laughing
at such a silly lass.

They went through the door as one,

flying hand in hand

into this world of wonder,

the fairies had a plan.

Daisy made a picture,

while Lexie wrote a note.

Daisy left a trinket-

a little seashell boat.

As quickly as they came,
the trio flew away.
The note they left had said
they would come another day.

Watching from safe distance,

their eyes upon the door,

they found their prayers were answered,

by flowers notes and more!

The children were excited

to meet these fairy friends.

"Oh yes," they said, "please visit."

And so this story ends…

Or is it just beginning?

So if you want the fairies

to travel through your door,

be sure to spread some kindness.

Give some, then get some more.

Do thoughtful little things
for friends and family too.
The fairies will take notice
and do the same for you!

We were just wondering...

- Which is your favorite fairy?
  Why?

- What picture do you think Daisy left for
  the children?

- How would you let the fairies know you
  wanted them to visit?

- What is something you have done today
  that would make a fairy happy?

- Has someone done something nice for
  you today?
  What was it?

Look for other books in
the Magic Door Stories series

About the Author

Laurie Ingersoll is an author and artist living on the lovely island of St. Croix. Look for her other books on amazon.com and laurieingersollbooks.com

Can you find St. Croix on a map?

Made in the USA
Charleston, SC
31 August 2015